Enchanted Lions

David T. Greenberg   ILLUSTRATED BY Kristina Swarner

DUTTON CHILDREN'S BOOKS

DUTTON CHILDREN'S BOOKS
A division of Penguin Young Readers Group

Published by the Penguin Group
Penguin Group (USA) Inc., 375 Hudson Street, New York, New York 10014, U.S.A.
Penguin Group (Canada), 90 Eglinton Avenue East, Suite 700, Toronto, Ontario M4P 2Y3, Canada
(a division of Pearson Penguin Canada Inc.)
Penguin Books Ltd, 80 Strand, London WC2R 0RL, England
Penguin Ireland, 25 St Stephen's Green, Dublin 2, Ireland (a division of Penguin Books Ltd)
Penguin Group (Australia), 250 Camberwell Road, Camberwell, Victoria 3124, Australia
(a division of Pearson Australia Group Pty Ltd)
Penguin Books India Pvt Ltd, 11 Community Centre, Panchsheel Park, New Delhi - 110 017, India
Penguin Group (NZ), 67 Apollo Drive, Rosedale, North Shore 0632, New Zealand
(a division of Pearson New Zealand Ltd)
Penguin Books (South Africa) (Pty) Ltd, 24 Sturdee Avenue, Rosebank, Johannesburg 2196, South Africa
Penguin Books Ltd, Registered Offices: 80 Strand, London WC2R 0RL, England

LIBRARY OF CONGRESS CATALOGING-IN-PUBLICATION DATA

Greenberg, David (David T.)
Enchanted lions / by David T. Greenberg; illustrated by Kristina Swarner.   p. cm.
Summary: One evening, Rose climbs on the back of an enchanted lion who takes her on a tour
of outer space, where they race with Monoceros the unicorn, pass by Pegasus and Pisces,
and are rescued from a black hole by Cetus the whale.
ISBN 978-0-525-47938-3
[1. Stories in rhyme. 2. Constellations—Fiction. 3. Outer space—Exploration—Fiction.]
I. Swarner, Kristina, ill. II. Title.
PZ8.3.G755Enc 2009   [E]—dc22   2008034215

Published in the United States by Dutton Children's Books
a division of Penguin Young Readers Group
345 Hudson Street, New York, New York 10014
www.penguin.com/youngreaders

Designed by Sara Reynolds and Abby Kuperstock

Manufactured in China • First Edition
1 3 5 7 9 10 8 6 4 2

To Ezra,
a lion most enchanted
LOVE,
DUVY

For Sara
K.S.

The sea is a maze of swirls;
The night is ablaze with pearls.
The blossoms of a pear tree
Suddenly rustle and sigh.

Heartbeat all aflutter,
Rose flings open her shutter.

Enchanted lions climb out of the sea
And shake their manes to dry.

They caper and slap,
Snarl and purr.
They nuzzle and nip
And lazily lick each other's fur.

Flopping onto the sand,
They start to wheezily doze.
Every lion but one, that is,
Who turns to look at Rose.

Rose stares back at the lion,
Beckons him in the gloom.

He flexes his claws and purrs,
And bounds into her room.

She scratches behind his ears.
He's magical (that's plain).

She climbs astride his back
And tightly grips his mane.

He snouts the curtains open;
Rose points up at the sky.

He tensely coils backward,
Leaps, and starts to fly.

The lion and his Rose
Swoop through outer space,
Past the giant rafters
Holding everything in place.

Past Pegasus, the horse,
And all his herd stampeding;
Past Pisces and her fish-kids,
Gluttonously feeding.

Past suns like Chinese lanterns,
Through galaxies they fly,
When Monoceros, the unicorn,
Abruptly gallops by.

Rose whispers to her lion,
Hugs him extra tight,
And the lion and the unicorn
Race across the night.

They jump-rope crescent moons,
Hopscotch asteroids.

They scamper and they frisk
Through interstellar voids.

Then suddenly they're yanked
By a cosmic suction cup.
They've trespassed a black hole.
It's vacuuming them up.

Rose creates a lasso
From a passing comet tail
And throws it over Cetus,
The mighty stellar whale.

Around her friend the unicorn
She loops her other arm.
Cetus beats his tail,
And pulls them all from harm.

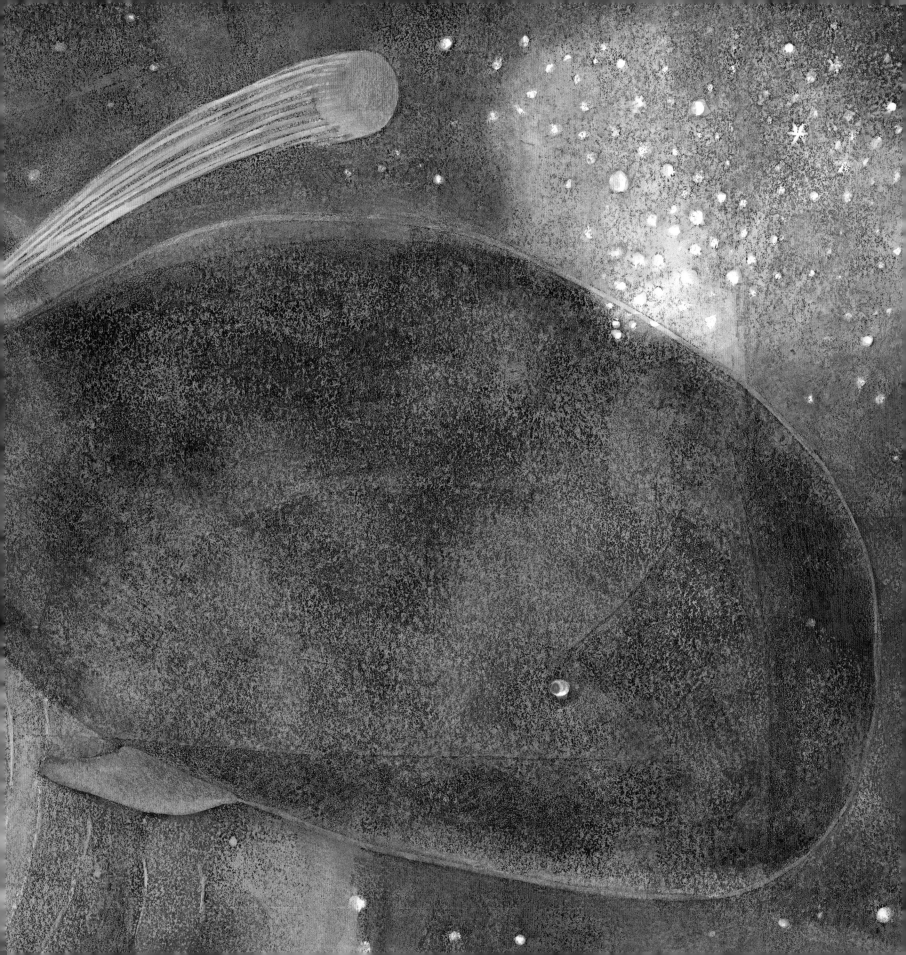

Home at last they zoom
To that isolated beach
Where every lion frolics now,
A happy kid with each.

The children kiss their lions,
Who lick them in reply.

Rose hugs her lion, strokes him,
Rubs noses, says good-bye.

She climbs back in the window,
Hears whispers from her tree,
Looks back, and all the lions
Are returning to the sea.

Rose falls fast asleep,

Having flown a million miles.

She tosses for a moment,

And then serenely smiles.